swamp

swamp

Ed Merwede

To order additional copies of this book, contact:
Xlibris
1-888-795-4274
www.Xlibris.com
Orders@Xlibris.com
776407

This book is dedicated to all those people

out there that have an imagination and

see and think things that they alone

create in their minds.

It is this imagination that brings their

dreams to reality and makes extraordinary

things come to be.

Think what the world would be like without

artists, architects, composers of music, scientists, and yes,

even writers. Living in a house without books is like

living in a house without windows.

Chapter One

Jake Wade, lieutenant detective on the Farmingdale Police Force, sat at his desk, feet up, reading the newspaper. He heard a knock on the glass and turned to see his chief motioning him in. *This can't be good,* thought Jake, *but it's the beginning of a new week and a new case.*

The chief said, "Sit down, Jake. I have a message to give you from a man called Hank Wilson, from New Orleans. You know him?"

Jake smiled and said, "You bet, Hank and I go back aways. Why did he call you instead of me?"

The chief said, "Because he wants me to give you permission to visit him in New Orleans. Business, not pleasure, and you were the only one he trusted to help him."

Jake hesitated and then said, "I've known Hank quite a few years, and if this weren't very serious, he would never have called."

The chief said, "I heard the same thing in his voice. Apparently, he can't trust any of his associates and is looking for help. Sounds serious. You have my permission if you choose to go."

Jake said, "Should I call him, or should you?"

The chief said, "It should be you, saying 'Hey, I have some vacation time. How about I visit you?' then even if his phones are tapped, you're clear."

"I like it," said Jake.

The next day, Jake made reservations for a flight into New Orleans. He had already spoken to his friend Hank and thanked him for the invitation to visit. Hank had said, "Anytime time, buddy, I'll pick you up at the airport."

When Jake arrived, there was Hank to help him get his bag and take him to his pickup. After getting in and closing each door, Jake said, "What's up? It doesn't sound good."

Hank nodded and said, "When we get back to my house, we'll have a long talk, OK?"

Jake said, "You got it."

They pulled into Hank's driveway, which was circular, and stopped at the front door. Jake got out, looked around, and let out a small whistle.

"It's better staying here than in the best hotel in New Orleans," said Jake.

Hank smiled and said, "It's a modest place I saved for years to own."

Jake started to laugh and said, "You old hound dog, you worked one hell of a deal to get this place."

"Well, it took a few years of wheeling and dealing, but the owner, who was getting on in years, was also a good friend, and we worked out a good retirement for him and a nice home for me."

After going inside, Jake said, "This place is beautiful. I'm very happy for you. The other big plus is, it's a waterfront property, right on a lake."

Hank said, "That's why you're here, the lake."

Jake put his finger upright between his lips and said, "Wonderful, let's go outside and take a look."

When they got outside, Jake motioned Hank over to the shore of the lake. Standing beside each other, Jake said, "Hank, I'm worried for you and whatever problem has developed here in your backyard. I've known you for years. We don't bullshit each other. Your asking me down here says volumes to me. You suspect something against the law, something big, is going on. That's why we are talking here at the shore. If the bad guys think you know something, they will start by tapping your phone, so do not say anything about what you think, out loud, in the house or on the phone, understand?"

Hank nodded and said, "Well, I'm not 100 percent sure, but my observations of one area of the swamp are very suspicious."

Jake said, "I'm tired from the travel. Let's have a few drinks, dine, and tomorrow, we go to work, OK?"

Hank patted him on the shoulder and said, "Good plan."

The next morning after breakfast, Hank and Jake walked down to the dock and got in Hank's boat.

Jake said, "Hey, what a beauty this is!"

Hank said, "Yeah, I picked it up about a year ago, very inexpensive buy. The guy was moving and just wanted to get rid of it." It was an eighteen-foot Boston Whaler with a 150 hp outboard motor.

As they pulled away from the dock, Hank said, "The river we want is about a mile away. It won't take too long."

He opened the throttle, and the bow rose for about thirty seconds and then planed off, the ride smooth as silk. As they approached their destination, Hank slowed way down, just creeping along, and said, "If we were to keep going, this lake connects with the gulf and the open water."

"How deep is it here and in the river?"

Hank said, "That's a good question. No one noticed, but at night, it must have been dredged to allow larger boats, because my depth finder says it's twenty feet from here all the way down the river. Never was before."

Jake said, "Are there any signs saying Keep Out?"

"Not that I've seen so far. But there are danger signs about an extremely large alligator roaming this entrance to the river. Some of the locals who have laughed at the sign came back terrified. Some didn't come back at all—their boats found drifting in the lake."

Jake said, "From what I understand about alligators, they do not attack boats."

Hank said, "Absolutely right, but the word around town is that this damn thing is prehistoric and very large. It even roars!"

Jake said, "You're right. Something that they don't want anyone to see is going down this river "

Hank nodded and said, "So what do we do?"

Jake said, "Let's take a look at the monster, and then we'll go from there."

Turning the boat toward the river and going slowly, they both kept their eyes on the shoreline for any movement. Then after going in about two hundred yards, they heard movement along the shoreline.

Hank had slowed the boat down—so slow they were just drifting about. As they were looking at both banks of the river, all was still, and then there was a very loud roar, and an alligator exposed itself through the weeds on the left bank. They both watched in amazement at the size of the beast and wondered what would come next. Hank started to turn the boat to leave, when Jake said, "No, just go a little farther downriver and see what our monster does."

They went a little farther, and the monster leaped from the grassy shoreline into the water.

Jake said, "OK, now change direction and let's leave."

Looking behind them, they saw a swirl of water following them. Hank hit the throttle, and they were back in the lake, just turning out of the entrance and heading for home.

Hank slowed to a cruising speed and said to Jake, "Now do you see what I mean?"

"Yes, I do, and on our next trip, we will eliminate the monster, which by the way is mechanical. I saw a wire attached, only briefly but I'm sure it was attached. On our next trip, we will put the mechanical guardian out of action."

Hank said, "Are you sure?"

Jake paused for a moment and then said, "Hank, once we take this first step, all hell will break loose. Are you ready for that?"

Hank laughed and said, "Jake, as long as I have you by my side, I'm ready for anything."

"Well, whatever is going on has been going on until now without any interference from the public or from the police. That disturbs me some. Either they made a deal with the chief, or he isn't doing his job. If you picked up on this, the chief had to know long before that. Now do you understand what we are up to?"

Hank said, "Yeah, I am, but to tell you the truth, I had no idea how big a deal this is."

Jake just smiled and said, "If it's drugs, we've got a war on our hands. I might have to call in reinforcements."

The next day, Jake said, "I have to make a few phone calls, and then I'd like you to give me a mini tour of the town so I get some feel for where I am, OK?"

Hank gave a thumbs-up and let Jake go to the phone. One minute later, Jake was back in the kitchen and said, "I almost broke my own rule. Phone might be tapped. I'll make my calls from my cell phone. Just stopped to show you how easy it is to make a mistake. It didn't hit me until I lifted the phone. Be right back."

Fifteen minutes later, Jake was back and said, "All went well. We should receive a FedEx package tomorrow, and then we'll be ready to go into action and find out what's going on, as they say, up the river."

The two of them left for a mini tour of the town. Jake said, "Can we stop by the police station so I can meet the chief?"

Hank smiled, shook his head, and said, "Be there in about five minutes. I have always found him as stern and not too talkative."

Not the best qualities for a chief, thought Jake.

When they arrived, Jake said, "I'll introduce myself and tell him why I'm here. You just back up my story, OK?"

Hank nodded, and then they both got out of the pickup and walked into the police station. They asked to speak to the chief and were told to wait while the secretary will see if he was available.

Jake whispered to Hank, "He's dying to see us, just wants us to wait. Watch, the answer is 'He's pretty busy, give him five minutes.' Bet you a buck."

His secretary came out and said, "He's pretty busy but wants to see you, just about five minutes."

Hank couldn't help it; he just started laughing and patted Jake on the back.

After maybe a little less than five minutes, the door to the chief's office opened, and he said, "Come right in, gentlemen."

"Thanks for taking the time to see us, Chief," said Jake. "You know my friend Hank here, but let me introduce myself. I'm Jake Wade, lieutenant detective, Police Department, Long Island, New York. I came down to visit my friend Hank here even though

I invited myself. Had some time coming to me and have never been here before."

The chief put out his hand and said, "Welcome, fellow police officer, glad to have you here and enjoy our beautiful town."

"I intend to. My friend here is giving me a quick tour today because I'd like to do some fishing. He lives right on the lake."

"Oh, I know where ol' Hank lives, been there quite a while. How's the fishing this year, Hank?"

Hank said, "So-so, but my friend here has that magic touch. He can find 'em whenever he goes."

"Well, I hope you boys enjoy yourselves and have good luck," said the chief.

Jake smiled and said, "I already picked out a good spot. We took a ride yesterday, and about a mile from Hank's place, there's a river on the right. Fish like intersections like that, maybe some big ones hiding in the river."

Jake could see a complete change in the chief's face, and then he said, "Well, your instincts might be right most of the time, but I'd stay away from that river. I've had reports of lots of alligators, and even a couple of fishermen go missing because of them, so enjoy yourselves, but please stay away from that river until I'm through investigating these stories, OK?"

Jake nodded and said, "Well, this is a great surprise for me. I haven't seen a live alligator. We might just take a peek and then get the hell out of there!"

The chief couldn't stop them legally, but it was as if he didn't like what he just heard. "Just stay safe, and please report to me anything unusual you come across, OK?"

"You bet," said Jake. "But alligators here are not unusual, are they?"

"You're right, just be careful. I have to attend to business now. Thanks for stopping by," said the chief.

Chapter Two

They left the police department and got in the pickup. After closing both doors, Jake said, "Whatever is going on up that river, the chief is in on it, too bad."

Hank said, "I've known him a long time. Are you sure?"

Jake turned to Hank and said, "I hope not, but right now, I'd put money on it. He's trying to increase his retirement. Bad news, but it happens."

They continued the short tour in silence until Jake said, "Hank, if you want me to leave rather than stir up the pot, just say so, no hard feelings. I know you have to go on living here."

"No, Jake, don't misinterpret my silence for wanting to quit. I'm just sorry for the police chief. Whoever is behind this got to him, and it had to be money. I've known him quite a while, and this is sad if true."

Jake said, "I understand, but after that package arrives tomorrow and we take that first step, there's no turning back. Chief's reputation or not, we find out what's going on. The chances are, we will be hit back softly after the first intrusion, and then we're on the dead list."

Around ten o'clock the next morning, FedEx delivered Jake's package. He took it into his bedroom and checked the contents.

Good, just as requested.

He came out, looked at Hank, and said, "Last chance to change your mind. I can't call in reinforcements until I'm positive there is a crime going on. That's what you and I are doing this morning, ready?"

Hank said, "I thought I was ready when I called you. I had no idea what would happen when you got here. Now I'm more interested and in total support of your plan. In other words, yeah! I'm with you!"

Jake was prepared for what was about to happen, but he was a little nervous about Hank, who had no experience in this sort of thing. Well, no turning back now.

They went down to Hank's boat about eight o'clock the next morning. The mist was just starting to lift, giving way to the sun. It was an absolutely beautiful view. They both got in the boat, and Hank warmed up the motor for a couple of minutes before casting off. They were both happy and anxiety ridden. They loved the day, being together, the thought of fish, but the knowledge of what their mission really was.

They rode in silence, knowing everything would change in a very short time. The river came into view, and Jake said, "Slow down and let's just creep in."

Hank cut the throttle and maintained just enough speed to control the craft. As they slowly turned and entered the river, Jake was getting one of his package requests ready. It was a tubelike device, much like a small bazooka. He loaded a small missile into firing position and waited. The wait was not long. The same enormous alligator slipped through the weeds and got ready to roar. That's when Jake took aim, waiting for the roar and a wide-open mouth. The roar came, and Jake fired a small missile directly into its open mouth. Phosphorus immediately turned the mechanical creature into white-hot flames. The heat was so intense the mechanical monster melted down to a pile of burned metal and exposed wires.

"Shall we proceed, my captain?" said Jake.

Hank was speechless, but he slowly started downriver. Then came a surprise. On the right bank of the river stood a black man with a machine gun. Jake said softly to Hank, "Ignore him, like we didn't see him."

The guard didn't like that and yelled, "You in the boat, stop now!"

Jake stood up and yelled, "Why? We're looking for fish."

The guard started to laugh and said, "Turn around, not even fish allowed down here."

Jake yelled back, "We're turning, but I'd like to talk to you. Don't go away. I'll be there in a minute."

The guard yelled, "You don't have to talk to me, just turn and leave."

Hank was just pulling up, bow on shore, when Jake jumped out. The guard turned the machine gun directly at Jake, but that didn't stop Jake. He kept walking up to the guard.

The guard yelled, "Stop! No farther."

Jake took two more steps, his hand extended, and said, "Calm down, man, that gun might go off! I just want to talk to you. Now point the gun down. You're scaring the shit out of me."

Hank couldn't believe that the guard actually pointed the gun down. He didn't take Jake's hand but did say, "OK, what do you want?"

Jake took two more steps forward and sat down on a tree stump.

The guard said, "What you want, man?"

Jake smiled, shook his head, and said, "Stay alive with you swinging that machine gun around. Put the damn thing down and let's talk, unless you're not allowed to. I came to catch fish, not be target practice for you."

The guard relaxed a little and said, "I'm hired so that no one goes any farther up the river, you understand?"

Jake said, "Yeah, I understand, but why? There's no law against fishing this river, and whoever is paying you does not own the water."

"Don't matter to me, man. They pay well, and I do my job."

Then Hank couldn't believe what he saw. Jake sprung up and, with one swift stroke, hit the guard in the throat. The machine gun dropped, and so did the guard, gasping for air. Jake was on him and handcuffed him in the blink of an eye. He picked up the machine gun and handed it to Hank. Then dragging the guard, he threw him in the boat.

"Let's head for home, partner. We caught the biggest fish I was after."

Hank backed off, turned the boat, and when he cleared the river, opened the throttle up for home.

On the way back, Jake used his cell phone to call the chief of police.

Hank said, "Is that wise?"

Jake replied, "You bet. He's going to take custody of our 'catch of the day' with charges I will state to the chief."

As they pulled up to the dock, the chief was there with one of his officers.

"What have you two been up to today? You were supposed to be fishing."

Jake jumped out of the boat and said to the chief, "Well, that's what we wanted to do, but things changed. First, we spotted a fire about a hundred yards into the river. We pulled in, but it was just smoldering by then, so we proceeded down the river and were stopped by the man handcuffed in our boat. No, *stopped* is too mild. We were threatened with death by machine gun if we went any farther. Luckily, we were able to overtake our assailant and bring him back here for you to make sure he is prosecuted to the full extent of the law. Parole should be denied. I examined his wallet, and he is an illegal immigrant, no visa card on him."

The chief stood dead still and expressionless while Jake was talking. The chief then said to his police officer, "Take custody of the suspect and put him in the van for transport back to the jail." With that, the chief turned to leave.

Jake said, "Chief, what do you make of this?"

The chief stopped and turned slowly to Hank and Jake. "I told you both to stay away from that river while I was investigating. You didn't take my advice. Now we'll see what happens."

"Whoa, slow down, Chief. We only responded to a suspected fire. The dude with the machine gun is a totally different situation. You have to agree."

The chief stood still and looked at both of them and then said, "Jake, you're a police officer and think you smell something bad. Leave it alone is the best advice I can give you."

All Jake said was, "Chief, don't throw away your career on this bullshit. You deserve better."

Chapter Three

A couple of days went by without incident. Hank and Jake took advantage of the time fishing and relaxing. They were sitting on Hank's porch, having a drink, when Jake said to Hank, "Hey, would you mind if I borrow your pickup tomorrow? Want to check a few things in town."

Hank said, "Great, would you mind if I came along? I have to go to the hardware and lumber store for some wood and screws. I have to fix the railing in the back of the house."

"That works out fine. While you're shopping, I could check out a couple of things. We could meet after, and I'll buy lunch. Whatta ya say?" said Jake.

"Sounds good to me," Hank replied.

The next morning after breakfast, they both got in the pickup and headed for town. They found a good parking space not too far from the lumberyard, and both got out to go their separate ways.

Jake said, "How about an hour and a half we meet back here, sound good?"

Hank nodded and was on his way.

Jake's first stop was the police station. He walked in and asked to see the chief. As the secretary started to say her rehearsed answer, the door opened and the chief stepped out.

Jake said, "Good morning, Chief. Seems like my timing was just right."

"Good morning," said the chief. "I wasn't expecting you."

"That's OK. I just stopped by to see how our prisoner is doing."

Chief shook his head and said, "Had to let him go. Nothing to hold him on. One of his friends stopped by and showed me his visa, which was legal, and said you approached him in a confrontational way. That's why he started to raise the machine gun. He said he would not press charges against you or the town. End of story."

Jake said, "You bought that bullshit because you are deeply involved. Shame, but you'll go down with the rest. I'm truly sorry for you, Chief."

The chief started to answer, his face bright red, but Jake was gone.

Jake walked down the street to the local breakfast shop. He walked in and noticed the place was empty. A waitress came out, and Jake said, "Are you open?"

She smiled and said, "You bet, it's just a little late. All the regulars were here as soon as we opened. We'll have a little pause before we serve lunch. What can I get you?"

Jake said, "Just a cup of coffee and a glazed doughnut, OK?"

"Comin' right up."

There were booths on both sides and tables in the middle. Jake took a booth near the rear. He was thinking about the chief and wondering how this was going to turn out when he noticed a black man coming through the door. As he stepped inside, he opened his coat, and Jake noticed the machine gun. Without hesitation, he dove under the tables in the center, just as the machine gun chewed up the table where he was and ripped the cushions apart. He rolled right and fired two shots into his assailant. The machine gun dropped, and the shooter went over backward, lying on the floor faceup. Jake immediately jumped up and moved to the back of the restaurant. His instinct proving true, the original gunman had a backup, who came barging out the kitchen door. Jake didn't hesitate; two shots put assailant number 2 down. He bounced off one of the tables in the center of the room, dropped his machine gun, and fell headfirst on the floor. Jake only paused for a second and then picked up shooter number 2's machine gun, turned, and ran out the back door. He came up the alley to the street, and there was the getaway car waiting. He walked up to the driver's door and tapped on the window. The driver jumped and reached for the .45 on the passenger seat. One burst from the machine gun and the side window exploded about the same time as the driver's head.

Jake walked back into the restaurant, took a seat, and said out loud, "Now I'll have my coffee and doughnut."

Nothing happened, and Jake knew why, so he got up and walked into the kitchen. They were all cuddled in a far corner. He said, "It's all over out there, no more shooting. Relax and compose yourselves. I would like a coffee and doughnut. Oh, whoever the owner is, the chief of police will be glad to pay for the damage done to your facility." It took five minutes to pour a cup of coffee and grab a doughnut, but at least, they were functioning again.

The waitress came out with his order, trying not to look at the dead shooter.

Jake said, "Thank you, and please relax. It's over."

She nodded, but she was still shaken to the boots.

The chief came running out of his office but slowed down when he saw the getaway car with blood splattered all over the windshield. He walked forward to the door of the restaurant. Opening the door slowly, he saw the first shooter lying just inside. He drew his gun and slowly opened the door all the way. He stepped inside, and the first thing he saw was the booth that had been ripped apart by machine gun fire. He stopped and looked all around. He spotted Jake in the last booth.

Jake said loudly, "Put away your gun, Mr. Peacekeeper of the Town. All the shooting is over. It's safe to come in."

The chief put his gun in his holster and sat down opposite Jake.

Before the chief could talk, Jake said, "The legal and upstanding visitor to our country, who you released yesterday because of his purity, came through the front door with a machine gun and opened fire. I was the target, but I dove under a table to protect myself. The shooter, I'm sure you know his name, hesitated before shooting again. That hesitation cost him his life; I shot him twice. His backup shooter came through the kitchen door, and I shot him twice before he knew where I was. I knew there was one more—the driver. I killed him. I was going to tell him the plot to kill me failed and he could go home, but he picked up a .45 handgun, and I was obliged to tell him that was a mistake, but he tried to point it at me. End of story."

"All I can say, Jake, is you should not have come here. You've stirred up a hornet's nest that will not settle down until you leave or stop poking around."

"Ah, just as I expected, a warning from their frontline of defense."

The chief's face turned red, and he said, "You know nothing at this point, nor how big an operation you have taken on. Back off, go home, and let it be."

Jake said, "That would please you no end. But you see, you're an officer of the law, and you have betrayed your oath. The good people of the town look up to you. You will go down in disgrace, mark my words."

"Only if you stick around and get lucky. This is big-time, you little shit, and there is no way you can win. Yeah, I'll retire very well, and not because of the meager pension offered me."

"I am now fully advised. I shall not stop, and when the chips are down, I'll be glad to put a bullet in you. Don't beg, remember that."

Jake walked out of the restaurant and met Hank coming down the street. He grabbed Hank by the arm and changed direction back to the pickup. They both got in, and Jake said, "I'm not sure you want me around anymore. They tried to kill me in the restaurant, but I survived. They will try again. Would you like me to leave, for your own safety?"

Hank said, "No, I invited you down because of this problem. It's like a virus, and eventually, it will take over the whole town. Please stay."

"You're a brave man, Hank, but as of now, we have to take precautions. We're vulnerable from the water and the land. It's my guess they will come from the water first. That's where we defend first."

Jake put in another call to his office, with a request for items he needed for the case he was on. No problem. The package, this time, was delivered by special messenger. Jake opened it and said to Hank, "Well, at least we're protected from a water assault."

They went down to the dock and, with Jake's knowledge, installed their defense system.

"Good," said Jake, "if they come by water, we'll know there here!"

Hank said, "You do know there are only two of us?"

Jake answered, "But we are smarter than they are. That's an advantage."

They worked for an hour until Jake said, "That ought to do it. Let's go back and relax until they make the next move."

Jake said to Hank, "I wonder why they are so intense on stopping us. Actually, we haven't seen a thing, except defense of the river."

Hank thought for a moment and then said, "Because if we go any further, we might see what they don't want us to see."

Jake said, "What if we see a big plant? We don't know what's going on inside. The average fisherman would ignore it and go on fishing. The plant is tucked away in the swamp. No one would logically go in there. Do you have a gun in the house? Any kind will do."

Hank nodded and went to get it. He came back with a twelve-gauge Remington pump shotgun.

Jake said, "That is absolutely perfect! I put trip wires by the dock and another a little way up the beach. If, or should I say when, they come, one of them has to set off an explosion. That's when we go into action. This is going to be hard for you. Just remember they want to kill you, it helps. When they come, it will be dark. I noticed you have floodlights on both sides of the house, facing the beach. Here's what we do upon the first explosion. Hopefully, they will only send four attackers. They have no idea what we've planned. When the first explosion goes off, and it will, we both run out the back door. You take the left side of the house, and I'll take the right. On my way out, I'll hit the switch for the floodlights. When you get to the back corner of the house, stay in the shadow. I'll be on the right side, and ready. Whoever is left will drop to the ground or rush for one of the sides of the house. *Do not* hesitate. Aim at his midsection and fire."

Hank said, "I hope I do my best. This is all new. I've never shot a person."

Jake said, "Do you want to die?"

Hank shook his head.

"Then fire without hesitation. These are bad people."

They had a before-dinner drink to calm their nerves and then had pasta carbonara, thanks to the talents of Hank.

Jake laughed and said, "Even if I die tonight, I'll die happy after that meal. We do not go to bed tonight. We can doze off in our chairs, but we have to be dressed and ready, OK?"

Hank just nodded consent.

Jake thought that if they were coming, it would probably be around midnight or a little later. They wanted Jake and Hank asleep and caught off guard. All the lights were out in the house, and the killers showed up at 10:30 p.m. For some reason, Jake woke up right before they arrived, and it being a moonlit night, he spotted their boat approaching the dock.

He ran and tapped Hank and said, "OK, ol' buddy, we're on. They just landed. Go and get in position. I'll hit the lights right after the first explosion. We now have the high ground, go!"

Jake watched out the window as the boat was tied up. He was right; there were four of them, and they stepped out of the boat very carefully so as not to make noise. They stood in a group, probably making plans, before they moved toward the house.

Walking very slowly, the first attacker inched toward the end of the dock, the rest close behind.

Good, thought Jake, *we might get two right off the bat.*

The first attacker reached the end of the dock, when his foot hit the trip wire. The explosion was quite large. Two attackers were down. The other two started to run forward when the floodlights went on. They both dove for the ground and stayed still for at least two minutes. Then one got up and decided to charge the house. He hit the second trip wire, and he was blown about twelve feet in the air. The third attacker got up and decided to take refuge on the side of the house. As he was running, he fired his machine gun randomly at the back of the house. Jake held his breath as the attacker got closer to the side of the house. With that, he heard the sound of the shotgun and saw the attacker blown off his feet. All was still, except for one attacker on the dock, who rolled over and tried to bring his machine gun up for defense. Jake, who at this time was approaching the dock, saw the movement and put three bullets into the attacker.

He then yelled to Hank, "All clear, buddy, come on down and join me."

Hank walked down, but he was shaking like a leaf.

Jake put his arms around him and said, "You did great, and we're both alive. Try to calm down. It's over for tonight. You go back in the house and fix a drink for both of us. I'll clean up here and be right in."

Jake picked up each of the bodies and dropped them in their boat. Untying the boat and turning it around, Jake got in and started the engine. Taking a rope, he tied the steering wheel to stay straight up the lake, threw the throttle in forward, and jumped out of the boat.

All in all, it was a nice night's work. *Oh, wait till the chief shows up tomorrow! Hank and I will plead innocent of any disturbance.*

Chapter Four

Jake got up early and walked down to the beach. He picked up the trip wires and then took the time to rake the beach. No wires, no holes where the explosives went off, and no footprints. He walked back to the house, put on the coffee, and started to make a nice big omelet for two.

Hank came yawning into the kitchen. Jake said, "Wait till you see what I have planned for today!"

Hank dropped down into a chair and said, "It better be peace and relaxation. Last night wore me out, not to mention scaring the living shit out of me! Can't take two of those in a row!"

"Nah, we sit still for a day and see where the shit hits the fan. But remember, *nothing* went on here last night, got it?"

Hank said, "Yeah, I got it, but why?"

"Because if I'm not mistaken, the chief is going to show up here pretty soon," said Jake, "and remember, we took them out so fast there isn't a bullet hole in the entire inside or outside of the house. Relax, we're clear."

Sure enough, fifteen minutes later, a car came skidding into the driveway. The chief jumped out, looked around, and then pounded on the door. Hank went to open the door and said, "Hey, what's with the pounding!"

The chief just looked at him and said, "You know damn well why I'm pounding."

He started to step in the house, and Hank said, "Do you mind asking if you can come in, or do you have a useless warrant?"

Jake thought, *Hooray for Hank. That stopped the chief in his tracks.*

The chief said, "Do you want me to go back and get a warrant?"

26

Hank said, "No, just slow down and tell me what the hell is going on. Oh, and yes, you may come in."

They walked into the kitchen, where Jake said, "Good morning, oh Peacekeeper of the Town, want some coffee? Sit down."

The chief was at the boiling point and didn't appreciate Jake's comment. "I prefer to stand, wiseass. And I have a few questions for the two of you."

"Go right ahead, Honest Abe, ask away," said Jake.

"You know, before this is over, I'm going to set you straight," said the chief.

Jake started to laugh and said, "My, oh my, you do remember straight. From what I've seen, that's amazing."

"OK, let's stop the shit. What went on here last night?"

Hank, bless him, said, "Well, Jake and I had before-dinner drinks, then a great supper of ribs, cleaned up, and played cribbage until we went to bed. I assume that didn't break any laws."

The chief said, "You wouldn't mind if we took a walk out to your dock, would you?"

Hank looked at Jake, and both of them said, "Why not?"

This stunned the chief because he was sure he would find shell casings and many other signs of an assault. They all got up and walked down to the dock. The chief was amazed. There was not a sign of any kind of a fight.

Jake said, "If you tell us what you're looking for, maybe we could help?"

The chief just stood there in bewilderment. *Not a sign of any kind.* He turned and said, "A boat was found pretty far down the lake, almost at the entrance to the river, and there were four dead bodies in that boat. The steering wheel was tied off for the boat to go straight. That's suspicious."

Jake said, "C'mon, Chief, fishermen do that all the time when they are trolling. How can that be suspicious? Now you have an empty boat with a steering wheel tied. What the hell has that got to do with Hank and I?"

The chief said, "Well, the boat wasn't quite empty."

Jake said, "Well, are you going to keep us waiting? How many fish did you get for dinner?"

The chief said, "There were four dead bodies in the boat."

Jake said, "Wow, that must have been one big fight for the fish. Shit, you take your fishing serious!"

They all walked back to the house, with the chief looking all around for just one small item to justify his visit. Nothing. They got to the back door and entered, when Jake said, "Does this mean every time there's a problem in or around town, you're coming out here to question us two desperadoes? You know there are laws against harassment, don't you? Or is all that legal shit not on your agenda anymore?" If the chief could have killed him, he was mad enough right then to do it. Jake wouldn't let go; he said, "Your face is as red as a baboon's ass. Calm yourself, or I'll call 911. Oh yeah, you're probably the 911 person who answers. See, that's the trouble with small towns. Well, I guess you'll have to save yourself. Is there anything Hank and I could do to make you more miserable? For some unknown reason, we're driving you batshit without cause. Why not sit down, have some coffee, while we smile and tell you what a shithead you are?"

The chief slammed his hand on the table and said, "You wiseass little prick, I'm going to enjoy putting you down!"

The chief turned to leave, when Jake said, "You better get out to that river and start kissing ass, because they are not going to be happy with you. In other words, they're not getting their money's worth."

The chief stormed out, slamming the door so hard it broke a pane of glass in the door.

"And now I shall have more fun," said Jake. "I'm going into town and getting someone to come out and replace that pane of glass. I will tell them to present the bill to the chief of police. They will probably object. I'll pay the bill and take it to the police station. I will not leave without a check."

Hank said, "You might be pushing too hard, don't you think?"

"No," said Jake, "the more we keep him off balance, the better we are."

Jake had measured the size of the piece of glass needed, and he took it to the local hardware and lumber store. He asked them to install it right away, even if it involved overtime. They said they would have it installed before the end of the day. Jake paid the bill and walked over to the police station. Going inside, he noticed the two deputies that worked for the chief put their heads down, as if they were busy with paperwork.

Jake walked over to the chief's secretary and said, "The chief, in his anger, broke the glass in our front door, so here is the bill for the replacement of that glass."

She looked up at him and said, "This is very unusual. I'll have to clear it with the chief."

Jake said, "I will not leave here without a check. I've already spent my own money to have it replaced."

She said, "Excuse me a minute. I have to check with the chief."

She knocked on the chief's door and heard a loud answer, "What?"

She opened the door and said to the chief, "Jake Wade is here and needs a check for the glass you broke when you left their house. Is it OK for me to write it?"

The chief came storming out and said, "Yeah! Write him a check."

Jake smiled and said, "By George, there is an honest bone in your head, thank you. Doesn't it make you feel good to be law-abiding?"

The chief, on the point of exploding, said, "Get out, Jake!"

Jake replied, "You bet, just as soon as I get my check!"

The chief looked at his secretary, who was obviously shaken by this entire interchange and fumbling to get the checkbook. She was so nervous at this point. She said, "Whom should I make it payable to?"

The chief, trying to contain himself, stood speechless. Jake said to her, "Please relax and make the check payable to me, Jake Wade, and we're finished." She looked at the chief, who nodded OK, and then wrote the check. She handed it to Jake, who not only took it but also kissed her hand and said, "Thank you."

Chapter Five

Jake drove directly back to Hank's home. Opening the door, he could hear the radio playing. Jake had never heard that before while in the house. He withdrew his weapon and, as silently as possible, walked toward the kitchen. Staying against the wall, he carefully peeked around into the kitchen. There was Hank at the sink, washing something and humming with the music. He stepped into the doorway and said, "Hank, I'm home."

Hank jumped and turned around, saying, "You scared the shit out of me. Make some noise when you come home so I know you're here."

Jake took a deep breath and said, "Hank, the rules of engagement have changed. Do you have an extra key that I could use? And from now on, keep all doors locked. Let's not make it easy for one of our intruders to get in quietly. As a matter of fact, later let's stop in town and pick up some bells, OK?"

Hank said, "Uh oh, you fired up the chief again, right?"

"He's so pissed he might come out here and shoot the two of us!"

Hank said, "Why are you getting him so riled up?"

Jake answered, "Mistakes are made when anger controls your thinking system. We can't go down the river anymore. At least not when they have guards watching and told to shoot and kill you know who. We lie low for a couple of days. That will worry them. Not knowing what we'll do next will start driving them crazy."

Jake thought for a moment and then said, "I wouldn't put it past the head honcho out there to tell the chief to take us out. They've been paying him, and now they want their money's worth. Oh, besides driving the chief nuts, I picked up some bear traps. We will place them together so we both know where they are, OK?"

Hank said, "This is much bigger than I thought. I shouldn't have gotten you involved."

"If you called anyone else, by now you'd be dead."

After dinner that night, the two of them went out and placed the bear traps.

"These are mean sons of bitches," said Hank.

Jake agreed, saying, "We want whoever steps on them to scream so we know they're here. I think we're OK for tonight, but I think the chief is having an extremely bad night."

Jake was right. The chief had arrived at the main building down the river and had gone inside, as requested. The man in charge was not happy. He told the chief to take a chair, which he did.

He walked over to the chair the chief was sitting in and said, "Do I have your attention?"

Before the chief could answer, he smacked him backhand across the face. Blood started to trickle down the chief's nose, but he remained silent.

"I'm beginning to get the feeling you're not worth the money we're paying, and that's bad."

The chief started to speak when the leader turned to him and shouted, "SHUT UP! From now on, you will keep those two assholes out of our business. Do you understand?"

The chief nodded.

"Oh, you poor thing, your nose is bleeding." He waved to one of his guards and said, "Bring my friend a clean cloth so he may wipe his nose."

The guard walked over and handed the chief a white cloth. Taking it, the chief wiped his nose and let out a loud scream.

The leader said that they had put medication on the cloth. The bottle had a diluted form of acid that would stop the bleeding.

"Sorry for your discomfort. But then again, do you realize the discomfort I'm in because of your failure?"

The leader, who answered to Gumbo, told his guard to take the chief and put him back in his boat. "Thank you for coming. I'll be in touch tomorrow. Oh, and I decided to hold this month's payment because of poor performance. See ya."

The next day was quiet because the chief called in sick. "I'll be back tomorrow, I hope. If anything requires my attention, you can call. See ya tomorrow."

The entire office was relieved. They suspected the chief was involved in something, and it was making the entire office uncomfortable

Hank and Jake hadn't made a move, just waiting to see what the opposition would do. It didn't take long. A lone assassin was sent out to eliminate both Hank and Jake. He was advised not to pull up to the dock, but to anchor the boat and swim ashore. He did and landed on the sand alongside the dock. Slowly he got up and began to move forward toward the house.

Lucky, he thought, *no lights went on.*

He ran to the corner of the house and stepped into one of the bear traps. He let out a roar that must have been heard a mile away. He was on the ground in agony when Jake showed up.

"Well, well, what vicious animal do we have here?"

The assassin pleaded for Jake to release the trap. Jake squatted down, picked up his machine gun, and asked, "Now why have you come knocking on our door?"

The intruder said, "Please, help me."

Jake said, "OK, and you please help me, OK?"

The intruder nodded. Jake released the trap and let the intruder catch his breath. There wasn't much fight left in him, but he tried to dive at Jake. It was a feeble effort, and Jake pushed him back down. Jake looked at him and said, "Do you remember our agreement?"

The intruder nodded.

With that, Jake picked up the trap, reloaded it, and said, "Stick out your left foot. I have a surprise for you."

"Please, please don't put that on again!"

"You're a liar, and I tried to help you. I'm going to ask you a few questions. If I think you're lying, then the trap goes over your head. Now, no more bullshit, just tell the truth. Do you agree? It's your neck."

Jake looked at him and said, "I'm going to ask you the first question. If you lie, there will be no second question. Do you understand?"

The intruder, in obvious pain, nodded agreement.

"Well, good so far," said Jake. "We will start easy, OK? Just tell the truth, or your head drops in the sand in front of you. What is your boss's name?"

The intruder said, "Gumbo. That's what everyone calls him."

Jake looked at him and picked up the trap.

The intruder yelled, "It's true, it's true! Everyone calls him that, very mean man."

Jake said, "OK, I believe you. Now you should understand I already know the answers to some questions, so be very careful. Next question is, What's inside the large building down the river?"

"Gumbo makes sure none of the guards, like me, go into a large section, which backs up to the water. Anyone who violates that rule is killed. I do know a good-sized boat comes in every two weeks, and no one except those whom Gumbo trusts help unload."

Jake said, "If you had to guess, what is unloaded?"

The intruder, with head down, said, "Drugs, absolutely sure."

"How come you're so sure?" said Jake.

"My brother-in-law works on the boat and slips me a sample or two."

Jake put out his hand and helped the intruder up.

"I'm taking you back in the house, where we will treat your wounded leg. There's a hitch, and you may make a choice."

When they got in the house, Hank met them and said, "What can I do?"

Jake said, "Get the first aid kit and let's clean up this wound and then bandage it so he doesn't get an infection."

Hank said, "That son of a bitch was sent here to kill us. Why the special treatment?"

Jake, looking at the intruder, asked, "Have you ever killed someone? Remember, truth."

No was the answer.

"I was not going to kill you. Was going to try and get away. I have a wife and children and want to bring them here."

Jake said to Hank, "If we can disguise him enough, I could arrange for him to be taken in custody in New York. He would be placed in a safe house, pending his testimony."

Hank said, "Why are you doing this for someone who signed on with killers?"

Jake said, "For two reasons. Number 1, I believe him about his wife and child, and also he's not a killer. Everyone deserves another chance—this is his." He then asked the hostage, "Do you understand what we're saying?"

He nodded and said, "Nobody give me another chance. I'm still nervous. I hope this is true."

Jake called his chief back on Long Island and made arrangements for the prisoner to be transferred directly into his custody. He said to Hank, "I'll be right back. Keep your eye on our visitor, oh, and he could probably use some food."

Hank said, "Sometimes, you surprise the living shit out of me."

Jake left and went directly to the Counsel on Aging and borrowed a wheelchair. Arriving back at Hank's house, he saw the chief's car parked outside. Jake got out of the car and went quickly into the house.

Hank said, "No surprise, the leader of the law-abiding citizens has paid us another visit."

The chief said, "Knock off the shit! I heard you two were attacked tonight."

Jake laughed and said, "Was that message sent to you by your boss on the river?"

"I have no 'boss' on the river as you say, but I do have informers that help once in a while."

Jake looked him straight in the eye and said, "What happened to your face? Nothing in the newspapers about any trouble in town that would cause your beating."

"I wasn't beaten, just had a bad fall, all my own fault."

Jake said, "Unless you fell into a fireplace, those are burns around your nose and mouth."

"I'm not here to answer your questions about my face. I'm here because I heard you were attacked tonight."

Jake said, "Here we are, law-abiding citizens, and you have the audacity to walk in here all beaten up and ask if we were attacked? It should be the other way around."

The chief, his face turning slightly redder than it already was, said, "Listen, smart-ass, you're in my jurisdiction, and I'm in charge. Now answer my question."

"This is so damn funny. I forgot the question. Do you mind repeating it?"

The chief said, "OK, we'll play it your way. I'll be back with a search warrant and find out what's going on in this house. Good night, gentlemen."

Jake, walking him to the door, said, "Would you mind telling us what you're looking for? We might be able to help."

The chief replied in anger, "You'll find out when I get back!"

Hank said, "What will we do with our prisoner?"

Jake said, "Easy. I'll tell him to wait in the woods until the search is over, and then we go back to plan A. The chief isn't going to look in the woods, and our prisoner has nothing to gain by trying to escape. I'll explain the whole thing to him right now."

Jake just got back in the house when the chief, with two deputies, showed up. They banged on the door, and the chief started to take a step in when Jake pushed him back and said, "You do not enter uninvited, and if you were crazy enough to get a search warrant, I would like to see it before you enter."

The chief handed him the search warrant, and Jake stood there, reading it.

"Well, well, well," Jake said to Hank. "It seems the judge didn't sign it. This is as false as our beloved chief."

The chief said, "That's a minor mistake. The warrant is still good, now step aside."

Jake, without a smile and dead serious, said, "You take one step inside this house, and I'll shoot you for breaking and entering."

Chapter Six

They all stood there without a sound. The deputies were visibly nervous.

"Plus, there's no reason on this warrant. I guess you forgot to tell the judge that it wasn't there." Jake handed it back to the chief and said, "Well, Wyatt, I guess the shoot-out at the not-so-OK corral has been postponed."

One of the deputies let out a chuckle that was answered by a swift disciplinary look and answer by the chief.

"You know, Chief, if you came here as a straight stand-up guy and a true policeman, we would have let you in and offered you coffee after your search. But you're dirtier than the edge of the swamp. Deputies, hold your position and comments. For the time being, you're still working for this, excuse the expression, chief."

The chief said, "OK, gentlemen, we go back to the station."

Jake went out and got the intruder out of the woods. The intruder was shaking with fear. Jake got him back in the house and gave him some food and hot coffee. He said to him, "Tomorrow, you leave here by plane. I will take you. You will be treated very well and put up in a house until we finish down here. Do not be afraid."

The next morning at the airport, a private jet landed, dropped the walkway, and waited for their passenger. Jake said to his prisoner, "Here we go. Nonstop, right onto the plane. Good luck, my friend." At that point, Jake wheeled him rather quickly to the awaiting jet. They helped him get aboard, closed the doors, and were ready for takeoff. The tower gave them clearance, and they were off.

The chief rushed in five minutes late, yelling, "CALL THAT FLIGHT BACK!"

The control tower informed him there was no reason to do so and that the flight was on its way.

Jake had watched as the chief's car skid to a stop with the chief running to stop the flight. As the jet turned and flew out of sight, he knew he had won a big plus in stopping the drug trade from up that river. They had a witness who had been inside and could tell the story of the plant, including murders and terrible punishments meted out by the head of the plant, known only as Gumbo.

Jake rode home to Hank's house and said as he walked in, "He's off and in good hands."

Hank asked if the chief had tried to interfere.

"Of course," said Jake, "but we were five minutes ahead of him."

Hank said, "What's our next move? We can't stand still. The chief doesn't know who was on that plane, but he does know it's bad news."

"Now," said Jake, "we really make it uncomfortable for Gumbo and the people who work in the plant. A series of incidents happening around the plant will make all workers nervous. And nervous workers will be a big problem for Gumbo. This will begin to drive him crazy and make him make a mistake. Once we identify the building as a confirmed drug supplier, we call in the Feds and give them our proof, and they will hit that plant and Gumbo with full force. Right now, it's you and I. Are you ready?"

Hank answered yes but said, "When I invited you down, I had no idea of the large scope of this operation."

Jake smiled, patted Hank on the back, and said, "That was a brave move by you. Once this ugly visitor is eliminated, you get your town back. Make no mistake, they would take over the town. They already got the chief of police, and that's just the beginning. It stops now. Just follow my lead, OK?"

Jake said to Hank, "If you had to guess, how far is it from where you turn into the river and where the building is?"

"Don't have to guess. I asked someone when they were building, and the answer was one-quarter mile."

Jake, rubbing his head, said, "That's a long quarter mile through that swamp."

"C'mon, Jake, you're not thinking of walking in. Or are you?"

Nodding, Jake said, "There's no other way. They would spot us right away if we went in by boat."

Hank said, "You're right, but that swamp is dangerous. All sorts of bad stuff in there. Alligators, snakes, spiders—you name it."

Jake laughed and said, "You're just trying to cheer me up, right?"

"We're about the same boot size. Do you have heavy leather boots? You know, the kind snakes can't bite through?"

Hank said, "Yeah, but I'm worried about you. I also have a compass and a large hunting knife."

"Night goggles would be great, but it's a full moon and clear weather, so I'm all set," said Jake. "Now we make plans and hope for the best. It's our only and probably last chance. You anchor just past the entrance to the river. I'm guessing, with any luck, about an hour to reach the building. I have a small evidence camera I can use. Is there any way I can let you know I'm on my way back?"

Hank said, "I have a flare gun on the boat for safety. There's only one white flare. All the rest are red and would catch attention."

"I'll take two reds and one white. The two reds I'll fire into their boat so they won't be able to use that or get out into the river. I'll fire the white straight up so you know I'm coming."

"Did it ever cross your mind that we're crazy?" asked Hank.

Smiling, Jake said, "Oh, only about five times so far." Not smiling, Jake said, "We go tomorrow, partner, and may the force be with us!"

The next morning, they both sat silently, eating breakfast. They were both thinking about that evening. They made sure the boat had enough gas. They checked the flare gun and decided where Jake would carry it.

"Does this thing still fire if it gets wet?" asked Jake.

"I wouldn't hold it underwater for any length of time, but yes, it's made to be waterproof," answered Hank.

"Oh," said Jake, "don't forget your shotgun and all the ammunition you have, OK?" Jake then said, "Bring a fishing pole and throw a line in the water, just in case you get a nosy visitor."

Jake said, "Hank, my buddy, I'm going to take a nap. It could be a long night, OK?"

Hank, smiling, said, "I'd wish you sweet dreams, but hopefully, that comes tomorrow."

Sunset occurred just around six o'clock in the evening, and Hank and Jake were in position at about five forty-five. They waited until just after sunset when Jake got ready to go. Hank pulled the boat up to shore and let Jake out in very shallow water. They both gave each other thumbs-up, and then Jake started his trek inland.

Jake kept his eyes peeled for holes filled with water, not knowing how deep they were. His progress was slow, but he was careful to pick his way forward. He wondered if they kept guards in the swamp, probably not realizing there were not too many idiots that would try that way. He got his answer sooner than he thought. He had just stepped up onto a mossy piece of land and was resting against a tree, when he heard a voice say, "Stand still or die right now!"

Jake turned and saw a guard with a machine gun standing about twenty feet away.

Jake replied, "I'm not moving, what's next?"

The guard started to answer when he shouted, "Damn! That hurt," and then looking down, said, "Oh shit," and dropped his machine gun. Jake walked over to see a water moccasin bite him again and then slip away.

Jake walked over to the guard, picked up his machine gun, and said, "Sorry, man, you got the wrong job. I'd help if I could, but I know nothing about snakebites. Hang on as best as you can." Jake continued on his way, now knowing they had guards spread all around.

Jake's progress was better than he thought, making good time toward his target. He spotted one more guard in front of him. This was going to be a nasty confrontation. The guard was leaning against a tree, smoking. Jake came up behind him and, withdrawing Hank's hunting knife, grabbed him from behind and quickly cut his throat. *Two down. Please no more to go.* After advancing another fifty yards, Jake could see the building.

OK, he thought, *now nice and slow, one mistake and I am dead.*

He got to the side of the building and inched his way to the corner. Carefully he peeked around the corner. He was just where he wanted to be. He could see the delivery boat and the loading platform. They were busy unloading one pallet of drugs after another. The boat was stripped down inside to accommodate four pallets of drugs. Then this good-sized man walked out and held his arms open. A woman, driving the boat, ran up, and they hugged.

That has to be Gumbo, thought Jake. One clean shot and he could take him out. But wait; he needed evidence to close this operation down.

The transfer finished; a worker moved the boat from the loading ramp and down to a small dock and tied it up.

Perfect, thought Jake. *Now, how to slip inside unobserved and get photos of the operation.* He tried a door next to the loading dock and found it open. They were lax at this time, because who could make it this far unobserved?

Chapter Seven

Jake opened the door very slowly, just enough to peer in. It was a short hallway, much like a vestibule, with another door at the far end. He stepped back outside and stepped into the shadows.

Sure enough, a guard came out, looked around, and yelled, "All clear, the door wasn't closed tight."

Fortunately, being a policeman, he knew how to jimmy these doors. He had to open it slowly and jam a stick in the hole very fast. That would show the door closed as long as it held. Jake stayed outside, looking around for the right something to jam the security device.

Jake jumped back into the shadows when he heard two voices coming close. They were guards coming off duty; he picked that up from their conversation. Jake took that as good news. The guards didn't think, nor did Gumbo, that anyone could get this far undetected, and surely they wouldn't be in that swamp at night. Jake worked his way around the building very carefully, checking if there was another way in.

Sure enough, he came to a window that let him look into the plant. He was amazed at the pallets of drugs stored along the walls. This he took a picture of. He kept going and came to an area at the back of the building that was surely built for Gumbo. There was an area cleared, walkways tiled, with gardens and flowers in between and surrounding the open area that was the patio of splendor. Tables, chairs, umbrellas, and lounges for the pleasure of His Highness, Gumbo.

Jake spotted the door that allowed entry to and exit from this patio. He decided not to try it, assuming it led to Gumbo's living quarters. He continued around the building, working his way back to where he came from. Then he spotted a cellar door recessed into the ground. He approached slowly and, as always, looked and listened for any movement. The doors were old and probably not used anymore. The question was, Were they part of the security system?

The problem with trying is you don't know until you're surrounded by bad guys. What to do? He checked the handles and hinges to see if the doors had even been opened in a while. They were covered by moss. It was decision time—try to open the doors and enter, but where to go from there? The door to the plant might be sealed. He kept going around the building, deciding his first choice was best.

He waited until all was still and most had gone to bed. He had found an old screw used when they built the building. This was a lucky find. After jamming it in, he could screw it in tight. His Leatherman knife had a screwdriver built in. He opened the door and jammed the screw in using the handle of his knife like a hammer, then he switched to the screwdriver to make sure it was anchored. He stepped back and waited. Nothing. The sweat was dripping in his eyes. A few steps forward and he got to the next door. Fortunately, the next door had a window in it. Jake leaned back against the wall to wipe his face and catch his breath. He carefully peeked inside. There was nobody around; their work for the day was done. Here came the big risk. Did the door he was at have a security lock? Didn't seem like it should, but now it was guess time.

Jake guessed no and hoped he was right. Slowly he turned the handle into the factory and then pushed the door open a little. He stood there, not moving an inch, and waited for an alarm. Nothing happened. He opened it just enough to squeeze in. Turning slowly, he took pictures of the entire inside of the factory. He was turning to leave, when he heard a door slam. The big man himself appeared at the far end of the factory where Jake had seen the outside patio. This was not good news. Jake slipped beside a pallet and held his breath.

Jake was wondering what spooked him. There were no alarms and no noise; thus, what made him come out, especially with a beautiful girl in his room? Dead silence. Then Jake heard his footfalls coming closer to the end of the factory.

"I know you're here. Come out, and we will talk nicely, OK?"

Jake took a small peek and could see the handgun in his hand. So much for talking nicely. He kept coming, and he was almost opposite the pallet where Jake was hiding behind. It was decision time. Jake decided to attack, because once Gumbo saw him, he was dead.

Three more steps and I go, thought Jake. *Hit him hard in the chest and knock the gun away. At least that would cut the odds some. This is one big son of a bitch.* One more step and Jake charged. He hit Gumbo solidly in the middle of his chest and swung hard at his wrist. Two things happened at once—one good, the other, so-so. The gun went sailing across the factory floor, which was a plus. It was highly polished, and the gun kept sliding quite away. The big man went down, but unfortunately, so did Jake. They both got up at the same time, but Gumbo was already running directly at Jake. Jake couldn't get his gun out and took a terrible hit. He went backpedaling about ten steps, almost lost his balance, but stayed upright.

Gumbo, like walking in for the kill, hit Jake with a blow on his left cheekbone and eye. Jake spun around, hit a pallet, and slowly turning, slid to the floor. Gumbo grabbed his ankles and dragged him almost to the center of the floor.

"And now, you bastard, you die. I am Gumbo, your executioner. Say goodbye, you shithead!"

Jake, semiconscious, was aware enough to know what was coming. Gumbo knelt down with one knee on either side of Jake's hips. "Oh, I am enjoying this."

Jake was still a little fuzzy from the beating, but the survival instinct and police training kicked in. He slid his hand to his side and removed the hunting knife Hank had given him. Gumbo was looking up and praising himself for the slaughter he was about to perform. Jake didn't hesitate; he swung his knife straightforward into Gumbo's midsection, pushing it in as far as it would go, and then drew the knife diagonally downward. This opened Gumbo's entire insides. He screamed, dropped his knife, and tried to get up. All failed; he fell sideways off Jake, writhing on the floor, blood pouring out.

Jake got to his feet and, stumbling, made it to the door. He went out, letting the door close silently, just as a guard entered the factory. Jake stayed against the wall in the lobby area, watching through the small window. He wasn't strong enough yet to try to escape, so he waited. The guard, seeing Gumbo cut and dead, wasn't sure what to do. Jake did.

He opened the outer door, knowing now that no alarm would sound, and started stumbling down to the dock. He approached very carefully, which was wise, because they had stationed a guard to sleep in the cabin. No wonder Gumbo was safe. He took every precaution to protect his job and the factory.

Approaching the dock, Jake noticed the guard slept with the cabin door open. Too bad. Jake took out his hunting knife, still covered with blood, and cut the mooring lines, setting the boat adrift. The guard did not wake up. He then loaded the flare gun with a red flare and fired it right into the cabin. There was a scream, and the guard came out, his clothes on fire. Jake shot him twice. *Now, please let me get back to Hank's boat.* The fire in the boat spread rapidly and inched its way into the gas tank.

Jake started to make his way back to Hank's boat and to safety. He guessed he had been walking about a half hour. He reached for the flare gun and fired one white flare into the clear skies. He kept on going, staying close to the river. That's when he heard a *toot, toot.* He looked toward the river, and there, like a vision, was Hank and his boat.

Jake waded to the boat, pulled himself over the side, and said, "Please let's go home." Saying that, Jake passed out.

Hank swung the boat around and opened it up, skimming across the lake without another boat in sight. That puzzled him because of the massive explosion when Jake's flare finally ignited the gas tank of the supply boat. Hank pulled up to his dock, tied his boat up, and then helped Jake into the house.

Jake sat down and said, "I really didn't think I'd be here again."

Hank said, "Let's have a small bite to eat and a large drink to follow."

Jake said, "Forgive me, I'll take the drink and then go to bed."

The next morning, Jake woke up and started to get up. That was when he became aware of all the pain in his body. He swung his legs out and just sat there, going over the events of last night. If it wasn't for Gumbo raising his head in victory and thanking whatever god he spoke to, Jake would be dead. Wow! The smallest mistake criminals make kills them. He wondered what was going on at the factory. That's when it dawned on him—someone at the factory must have called the supplier and reported the disaster. They would take action immediately and try to empty the factory and save the drugs. Thus, Jake walked as fast as he could to the telephone. He called his chief and brought him up to date on what happened and about the photos he had.

Jake said to the chief, "When you alert the FBI, how fast will they get here?"

The chief said, "Can you fax me the photos? They'll be there tomorrow, I hope."

Jake said, "The photos are on a digital chip, and I don't know any camera shops here I can trust. What if I just send you the chip through FedEx, and you take it from there?"

The chief said, "Fine, but that adds one more day, you realize."

"OK," said Jake, "one day and one day only, or yours truly is dead. I think I can stall them one day, but that's the limit."

Jake looked at himself in the mirror and decided Hank should go into town with the chip and send it through FedEx.

"Shit," said Jake. "That bastard Gumbo really hit me hard. The left side of my face is completely black-and-blue, and my eye is just starting to open." He walked into the kitchen to find Hank had already made him a ham-and-cheese omelet. Jake sat down and said, "Hank, you are surely a blessing. I'm starved."

Hank looked at him and said, "It's a wonder you're still alive, my friend."

Jake just nodded. He wolfed down the omelet and was relaxing. He was having his coffee when he said to Hank, "I have a job for you, if you're agreeable."

Hank sat down with Jake and said, "What is it, my friend? I'd be glad to help."

Jake told him about the phone call and sending the photo chip from his camera via FedEx.

Hank said, "No problem. I know the guy at FedEx, and the package will be on its way immediately."

Jake said, "Whatever the cost for the fastest delivery is fine. You will be reimbursed. Unfortunately, you and I have another job, if you're still in the game?"

Hank laughed and said, "How can I stop now? Of course I'm in."

Jake said, "This might not be too easy. We have to stop another boat from entering the river."

Chapter Eight

What Jake didn't consider was, the warehouse was just a supply station. They held quite a large storage and shipped out by demand. The supplier to that warehouse was in Colombia. They made sure there was enough product on hand at that station to fill all orders within that locale. So Gumbo would advise them of the orders he had standing, how much he had on hand to fill that order, and how much more product he would need to be ready for other orders.

Gumbo's warehouse had just been replenished, which meant he had a full warehouse. This was not to be lost. A boat was ordered to leave immediately and retrieve the contents of that warehouse. Failure was not an excuse. The boat they sent was large enough to take on all the drugs from the ex-Gumbo plant and was armed enough to withstand any assault from that area. Responding as fast as they did, they didn't think the FBI could possibly respond any faster. They should be at least two days ahead of them.

"OK, Hank, we have a small problem on our hands. The bad guys are going to try and empty that warehouse before the Feds show up. That means they have already launched a boat large enough to hold the inventory at the warehouse. It will be armed, but not to the hilt. They do not expect too much resistance, being the first ones to arrive. That's where we come in."

"Oh great," said Hank. "How the hell are we going to stop a boat twice our size and armed to the hilt?"

Jake said, "Relax, I'm working on it."

"Now that gives me a lot of confidence. You came back from our last assault half alive, and now you're ready to go again?"

Jake smiled a crooked smile and said, "Are you with me? I will come up with a plan."

"Hank, do you know a place in this area that sells dynamite?"

Hank said, "Yeah, it's about an hour from here, but I know the owner. I bought some to clear the beach when I moved in."

Jake just looked at him and said, "My friend, you just might have saved the massive distribution of drugs." Jake walked over to him and gave him a bear hug. "Let's go. We don't have much time."

They got in Hank's pickup and started up the drive. They turned onto the main road and were on their way. The chief of police went speeding by, siren blaring.

Jake said, "There is a man in panic. I bet he's going to your house for something."

Hank said, "That poor bastard made a deal with the devil and now is in a panic for he knows the results of failure."

Jake smiled and said, "You're really catching on to this game."

They pulled into an industrial park that sold different grades of sand, blue stone, many different sizes of cobblestone, brick, etc. Hank pulled up to the shack, which was the main office, and stopped.

"Let's go," said Hank. "You tell him what you want, and I'll vouch for you."

"Do they honor police badges?"

Hank said, "That's the last thing we use if he won't sell us what we want, OK?"

Jake nodded and followed Hank into the office.

"Hank, old buddy, haven't seen you since you cleared your beach. Whatever brings you here, I'll be glad to help."

Hank shook hands with the owner and then introduced Jake as a good friend he'd known for years.

"Great," said the owner, "Nice to meet any friend of Hank's."

Jake shook his hands and said, "Thank you. Believe me, I appreciate it."

The owner then said, "Wow! What does the other guy look like?" He obviously was commenting on Jake's face.

"Not so good as it turns out."

"Well, what can I do for you two fellas?"

Hank said, "I want to buy three sticks of dynamite for a project I have. Is that OK?"

The owner said, "For you, no questions asked. Just don't hurt yourself. I can't find new friends that easy anymore."

With that, he got up and was gone for about two minutes, and then he came back with the three sticks of dynamite.

"I'll send you a bill. No cash dealings happen here."

Jake stepped forward and said, "You have no idea what you just helped Hank and I with, but you will in the future, and probably get an award for your service."

The owner just looked at both of them and said, "Good luck, gentlemen. May your plans work out."

They both went out and got in Hank's pickup. They pulled out of the parking area and headed for Hank's house.

Jake said, "Let's hope the chief is still not there."

Hank said, "Good question. Maybe we should hide the dynamite. That bastard is running wild right now. Anything he finds is a plus to save his ass."

"Good thinking, Hank. Where can we put the dynamite that he can't find it?"

"Right in front of his eyes. I'm going to stop and buy some groceries. We just put them at the bottom of the bag."

He received a thumbs-up from Jake. After the stop at the grocery store, they headed home. Sure enough, the chief's car was parked outside. Hank parked his truck, handed the grocery bag to Jake, and got out. Jake followed from the other side. The chief opened his door and got out. Then the other door opened, and one of the guards at the warehouse stepped out.

Jake said, "You're keeping bad company, Chief."

The chief said, "Just be quiet and answer my questions."

Jake said, "Why? You have no right to question us."

The chief said, "Yes, I can ask you questions because I have an eyewitness to what you did last night."

Jake smiled and said, "Exactly who is your eyewitness?"

The chief waved to the guard to step forward. He did, but very reluctantly. He stood alongside the chief but was silent.

Jake's eyes bored into him, and he said, "Well, exactly what do you think you saw?"

He was very nervous and hesitated to say anything. The chief nudged him and said, "Now is the time to speak. Do you know what I mean?"

The guard said, "Yes, I know what you mean, but today is different from yesterday. Gumbo is dead."

The chief was filled with anger at this point and said, "Remember, you're in my custody, and you will suffer the penalty of the law for not answering truthfully!"

Jake looked at the guard and said, "At this point, you have not committed a crime. Do not let the chief bully you into something that will cause you harm. Remember, the chief worked for the now-dead Gumbo. Be careful what you say."

The chief, almost exploding with anger, said, "Look, you lowly hunk of shit, say what we talked about in the station!"

The guard, now so nervous, could hardly say anything and just stood dead silent.

"Tell them what you told me, and damn it, do it now or I'll put you in jail!"

"Stop!" yelled Jake. "That's against the law, and the chief knows it. You will not go to jail." Jake then said to the chief, "Is he under arrest for anything?"

"No, not at this time."

Jake looked at Hank and said, "Let's invite him to dinner tonight. It looks like he could use a good meal. No problem there, right, Chief?"

The chief turned around and got in his car. He pulled up a little, rolled down his window, and said, "You two have no idea what you have caused. It's bigger than both of you. We may not see each other again."

"I wonder want he meant by that?" asked Hank.

Jake said, "They're running scared and will try to eliminate anyone who could identify them or anyone responsible for the closing of their location here, which is very profitable."

Hank said, "The chief must be very nervous right now. He accepted money to keep the river clear and failed. That's a very serious violation. His days are numbered."

Jake said to Hank, "We can continue this conversation later. Right now, I think you and I and our guest should eat."

The guard was very nervous and afraid he would be killed.

Jake said to the guard, "Relax, please, we will not hurt you. As a matter of fact, we are preparing a good dinner for you."

The guard, still nervous, said, "Why are you treating me well? I was a guard for the plant."

"How many people have you killed in your job?"

"None. I don't believe in killing. I took this job to feed my family. That's all I wanted to do. Gumbo was very strict and made us take target practice twice a week. Sometimes on targets and sometimes on real people—derelicts he would pick up in town. I never was asked to do that. Otherwise, I would not be here. Those that hesitated to shoot and kill were told to walk forward and take the place of the derelict. Gumbo then walked into the position they were in and said to all of us, 'This is the way you kill an intruder.' With that, he would raise his machine gun and shoot the poor man to pieces. At that point, he would say, 'Lesson over, I hope you all learned something. For if you hesitate and let an intruder through, you will be the subject of my next training session.'"

The guard said he wished he could escape and not be part of that ugly operation.

Jake said, "Obviously, there was no way possible to refuse, right?"

The guard said, "Gumbo was feared by everyone in my village, and we all hoped he would not show up looking for men to add to his small army. He would drive up and down the streets, looking. If he spotted a young man, one of his trusted guards would bring him to Gumbo's car. Gumbo would ask if they were married. If they said yes, Gumbo would smile and tell them they are now, as of this minute, hired as a guard. Then he would add, 'You can say no, but then your wife and any children you have would be killed.' How do you answer? That's why I'm here. It is a great relief knowing that Gumbo is dead and my family is safe."

Jake and Hank took another guard prisoner and put him away in hiding after he agreed to testify about what was going on in that plant.

"How do you feel about that? And of course, tell the story you just told us. With any luck, we will try to reunite you with your family."

The guard lit up and said, "Yes, of course. I want to see my family again."

"Are there any new guards, like you and the other guard, that want out?"

"Oh, no, all the rest are Gumbo followers and vicious killers and will fight to the death to protect that factory before they remove all the drugs."

"Did you hear anything about how they will transport all the drugs?"

"Yes. After your first small attack—getting rid of the mechanical alligator and killing one of his guards—he was furious. According to some of his hard-core guards, who spoke openly in our small quarters so I heard, it was to be by boat, which is large enough to hold his entire inventory. Some of the guards were glad to be picked to guard the entrance to the river, three on each side. Each one is hoping to replace Gumbo because of their bravery."

Jake arranged for another police helicopter to take this guard and place him with the other one.

Chapter Nine

"Now we have a problem," said Jake. "Six guards, three on each side of the river, the boat coming in, and there is just two of us."

Hank said, "Well, we tried, and they will be out of here. I guess we have to settle for that."

Jake, pacing back and forth in the kitchen, kept saying, "Damn, damn, damn, I will not lose when we're this close. Those drugs have to be stopped. I refuse to lose at this point without one hell of a fight! How many fishermen do you know in this town—friends, I mean?" he asked Hank.

"About four trustworthy, stand-up guys."

"Can you call them and ask them to come here tonight, very important."

Hank said, "I'll try."

When Hank got off the phone, he smiled and said, "All four will be here in an hour."

Just about an hour later, they showed up, one after another. When they were all settled, Jake laid out the situation—from beginning up to the present, including the police chief being in on it and taking money to keep the river off bounds. Knowing the whole situation, Jake asked, "Who among you is willing to stop this drug run?"

Two of the four stood up and said, "We're marines. We know how to fight and would not hesitate to take out a few enemy guards."

Jake said, "Wow! We're lucky to have two ex-marines with us."

Billy, one of the two that stood up, said, "There's no such thing as an ex-marine."

The other two said, "We want to help. What should we do?"

Jake said, "Look like you're just fishing, but if you own any type of gun, like a shotgun, bring that along. Believe me, you'll know when to use it."

Hank added, "And handguns are helpful also. Bring ammunition and whatever weapons you have."

"Now, Jake will lay out the plan. We stick with it, and all hell will break loose. They will learn that honest men are much stronger than they think."

Jake said, "We have to get there first, before the guards take their position and before the boat comes into sight."

Billy, one of the marines, said, "Erich and I have to be dropped off, one on each side of the river. That way the guards will be taken down before the boat is too close to hear anything. If all goes well, nobody will hear anything."

Jake said, "Done. We meet at the end of the river at five thirty. Is that good?"

All agreed. The meeting was over, and everyone left.

Hank and Jake sat at the kitchen and had a drink before going to bed.

Jake said, "Did you know Billy and Erich were marines?"

Hank said, "I had no idea, but how lucky are we to have them with us?"

"Tomorrow will tell, but I'm glad they're with us."

The next morning, Hank and Jake headed out early; they wanted to be there before anyone else. When they arrived, a boat at the shore came out to greet them. It was the two marines, dressed in camouflage uniform and belts both with handguns and hunting knives, their faces blackened.

Billy said, "I'm taking the right corner of the river, and Erich will take the boat and the left corner of the river. He will hide the boat. Good luck to all of us, and may we celebrate afterward."

With that, they were gone.

"Hank, my buddy, you picked two winners. They will neutralize the sides of the river. After that, it's up to us to stop the boat. Good luck, my friend, just do the best we can."

They dropped anchor, blocking the entrance to the river, and started fishing. When they saw the other boat pull up alongside, one of them said, "Where do you want us?"

Jake said, "Do you have weapons?" They both held up twelve-gauge pump shotguns. "Great, when we hit the boat, start shooting at anyone you see on that boat."

"Well, we're as ready as we can be with our ragtag army. These are brave men. Let's hope we succeed."

Hank spotted a small speck on the horizon, took out his binoculars, and said, "It looks like our visitors are approaching."

Jake said, "Good, keep an eye on them. That means the guards are either in place or about to be."

There was dead silence from both sides of the river. Hank and Jake didn't know whether that was bad or good. That's when they heard two handgun shots from the right shore. Jake said, "I think that's good. The guards use machine guns."

Jake was right; the camouflaged marine on the right shore of the river had just taken down both guards. Then they heard one shot from the left shore. This bothered them both until they saw the other marine pull his boat out of hiding and head toward his buddy on the other shore. Surprisingly, he came to the edge of the river and jumped in with his pal. They motored out to Hank, and Jake and said, "The guards are no more. We're heading down the river out of sight. If they get past you for any reason, we'll do our best to cripple them. Good luck."

Hank watched them with his binoculars and then put the binoculars away.

Jake said, "Why put the binoculars away?"

Hank said, "Because if I can see them, they can see us, and we don't want to look suspicious, do we?"

Jake said, "Hank, you really have gotten into this operation."

The boat was now approaching the river's entrance, which was blocked by Hank and Jake. They blew their horn and threw the boat in reverse until the entrance was cleared.

On the bullhorn, a voice said, "You are blocking our way, please move."

Jake stood up and said, "Will do. Just give us a minute."

With that, Hank yelled, "I got one on!" his pole bent in half. Hank kept reeling and couldn't believe even the fish were helping. Hank brought the fish in and held it up for all to see.

Jake stood up and said, "OK, we will pull anchor and give you entrance. Thank you for your patience. Would anyone on your boat like a nice fresh fish for supper?"

"Yeah, man, haven't had good fish in a while."

Jake smiled and said, "No problem, we'll pull alongside and throw the fish up."

While Hank was pulling the anchor, Jake got the dynamite ready. They would both throw at the same time and then motor as fast as possible to the other side of the boat, throwing one more stick of dynamite. Then if the men on the boat were still alive, they would motor to the bow and throw one more stick. The men had forgotten about the other two fishermen. They came straight from behind the boat, and both opened fire with their shotguns. Two guards, just running up on deck, caught both blasts and went down. Hank and Jake made it to the bow and threw the last stick of dynamite. That blew out the windshield and killed the captain. The boat was now barely afloat and with no captain. If anyone was left alive, it would be a miracle.

Jake, Hank, and all the rest of their team pulled up alongside the crippled ship.

Jake said, "I organized this party. I'll climb aboard and see what's left, just standby for me to return, OK?"

All agreed, and Jake jumped on the swimming platform and slowly peeked over the edge. There were lots of smoke and debris, and about four guards were lying on the deck. Slowly, without taking his eyes off the cabin, he slid over the side. Jake walked forward very slowly, watching for movement from anywhere. He saw the captain's seat with the captain lying alongside it. He was dead. Still moving forward, Jake saw his first mate, or what was left of him, also lying in the cabin. He looked around, and no one was left moving.

Jake walked to the stern of the boat and asked the two marines to come aboard. They both tied their boat to the cleat on the larger boat and then climbed aboard.

After they were both aboard, one said, "What's up, Jake?"

Jake took them forward and showed them the hatch and said, "That bothers me. No telling what's below. How would you treat this?"

Billy said, "I'll take one side, and Erich will take the other. All you have to do is stand behind the hatch and slowly open it."

All agreed, and Jake attached a line to the handle so he could stand back and open the hatch all the way. They all nodded, and Jake started pulling. The hatch opened a crack at a time until it was fully open. Nothing happened, no one came up, and no one fired any shots.

Both marines said, "We wait just a few minutes and then go down."

There was residual smoke coming out of the hatch, but not enough to block their view. Erich nodded to Billy and started down the ladder to the hull. No noise.

Then Erich called up, "All clear, this you've got to see."

Billy and Jake made their way down the ladder and looked around.

The entire hull of the ship was lined with steel and completely empty to receive all the drug pallets at the factory. There wasn't any place for someone to hide; it was that barren. They went back up the ladder, one at a time, and then closed the hatch. They shook hands, and Jake decided their next move.

After getting in their respective boats, they all raised their hands in salute of a good operation.

One of the marines said to Jake, "You're a great leader. I'd follow you into any situation."

Everyone clapped. Jake said, "OK, now comes the wrap-up. I'm putting in a call to the chief of police and ask him to come out here. We have a problem."

They all sat down, smiling.

Chapter Ten

They all sat there, anchored around the main vessel, waiting for the police chief to arrive.

One of the marines said loudly, "Our adversary, the dishonorable chief, is approaching."

Jake said to all, "Let's stand up and salute."

The chief, with one deputy, slowed down and pulled up alongside Hank and Jake.

"You two are in serious trouble. I want you to drop your weapons right now!"

Jake, smiling and shaking his head, said, "How can you have the audacity to arrive here, one of the bad guys we've been fighting to stop spreading drugs, and ask us to drop our weapons? As of this minute, you are one of the last persons involved in this drug operation, and I would suggest that you immediately drop your weapon or be blown to hell where you stand."

The chief looked around and saw every weapon was pointed at him. He stood dead still without saying a word and reached for his sidearm. He could not help but hear several guns being cocked. He slowly removed his sidearm, raised it to his mouth, and fired. His deputy raised his arms above his head.

Before the end of the day, the FBI had landed helicopters and had agents going through the entire plant. They also towed what was left of the vessel that was supposed to empty the warehouse. Records found in the plant were sufficient in shutting down several drug dealers in Florida.

The chief's deputy was found not guilty and was returned to his job. Little did he know at that time, the town voted him in as chief.

The two fishermen that supported the assault on the boat and, of course, the two marines were invited to a grand cookout at Hank's house—clams, crawfish, shrimp, lobster, and corn on the cob, not to mention a goodly supply of beer.

The next morning, as Jake was putting his luggage in the car, he turned and saw Hank approaching him. Jake put out his hand and shook Hank's, then stepping forward, he gave him a hug and a pat on the back, saying, "Hank, you are one good man who has attracted wonderful stick-by-you friends. You're a lucky man, and if you ever need my support again, you know where I am. I understand there is quite a reward for Gumbo. It's all yours. Maybe buy a new boat, and next time I come down, we really fish."

Hank said his goodbyes and waved as Jake took off for home.

The following week, the new chief of police and most of the shopkeepers kept shaking Hank's hand and saying, "Thank you. Our town is better off for your bravery."

Hank went to the new chief of police and said, "Why don't you have a meeting with the town officials and organize a town fair? Everybody that comes brings something. I'll supply the beer and the hotdogs. I think we all need to come together and celebrate the closing of that drug plant. It would have ruined this town. Whatta ya say, Chief?"

"Consider it done, Hank, and if your friend Jake could fly in, it would make it special."

Printed in the United States
By Bookmasters